For Jess, my very special daughter – E.W.

For all my friends, for being Just So wonderful – M.A.

Thank you to our editor Emily Ford
and designer Lorna Scobie.

First published 2017 by Macmillan Children's Books
an imprint of Pan Macmillan
20 New Wharf Road, London N1 9RR
Associated companies throughout the world
www.panmacmillan.com

ISBN: 978-1-5098-1474-9

1 3 5 7 9 8 6 4 2

A CIP catalogue record for this book is available from the British Library.

Printed in China

Rudyard Kipling's

JUST SO STORIES

Retold by Elli Woollard
Illustrated by Marta Altés

MACMILLAN CHILDREN'S BOOKS

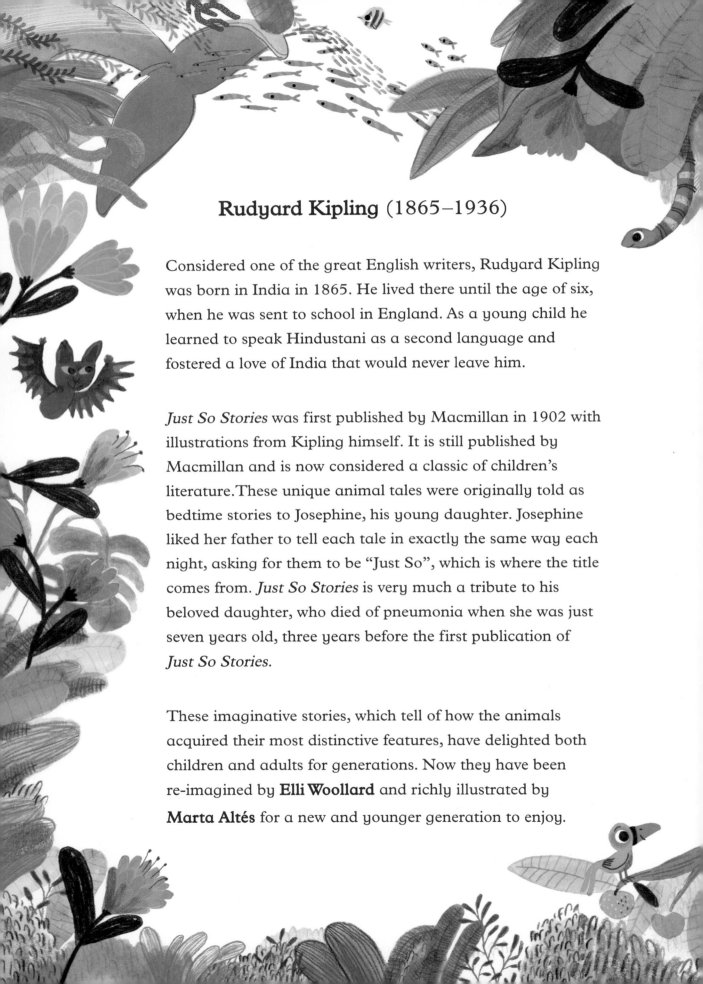

Rudyard Kipling (1865–1936)

Considered one of the great English writers, Rudyard Kipling was born in India in 1865. He lived there until the age of six, when he was sent to school in England. As a young child he learned to speak Hindustani as a second language and fostered a love of India that would never leave him.

Just So Stories was first published by Macmillan in 1902 with illustrations from Kipling himself. It is still published by Macmillan and is now considered a classic of children's literature. These unique animal tales were originally told as bedtime stories to Josephine, his young daughter. Josephine liked her father to tell each tale in exactly the same way each night, asking for them to be "Just So", which is where the title comes from. *Just So Stories* is very much a tribute to his beloved daughter, who died of pneumonia when she was just seven years old, three years before the first publication of *Just So Stories*.

These imaginative stories, which tell of how the animals acquired their most distinctive features, have delighted both children and adults for generations. Now they have been re-imagined by **Elli Woollard** and richly illustrated by **Marta Altés** for a new and younger generation to enjoy.

Contents

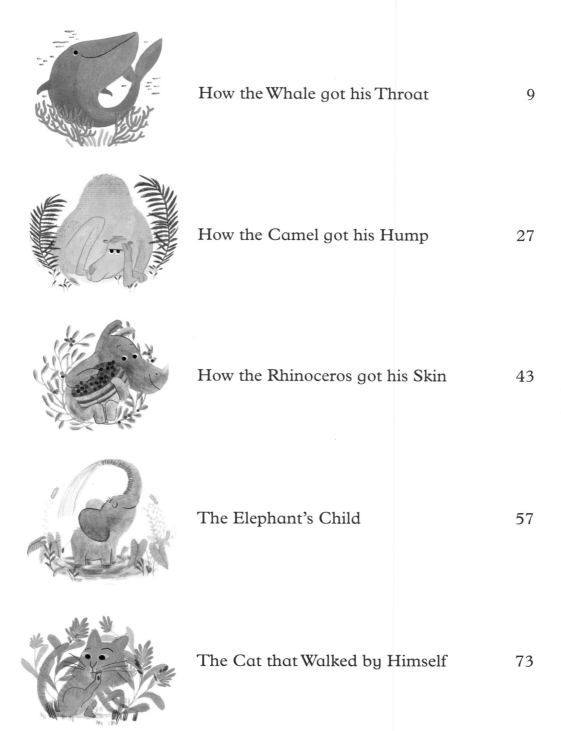

How the Whale got his Throat

This is the tale of how whopping huge whales,
Who have mouths that are bigger than boats,
Cannot eat a child that they find in the wild,
As they have the most teeniest throats.

The Whale was a beast whose great joy was to feast
On the tastiest things in the sea.
If he wished for some fish, then his tail would go *swish!*
And he'd gulp them all up for his tea.

"The skate and his mate," sang the Whale, "both taste great,
   And the swirliest, twirliest eels,

The dab and the garfish, the crab and the starfish,
   They all make such marvellous good meals!"

So he gobbled the dace, and he guzzled the plaice,
And he gorged and he gulped, on and on.

Then one day he cried, "I feel empty inside!
But those fishies all seem to be . . .

. . . gone!"

Whale swam through the waves,
    searching coral and caves,
And he hunted for fish half the night

Through seas that were hot,
    and through seas that were not,
But there wasn't a fish left in sight!

"The skate and his mate,"
    sang the Whale, "both taste great!
Yet it seems I have eaten them all . . .

But still, here is one, and it's better than none.
Though it seems most exceedingly small."

"Fishy, my dear," said the Whale,
   "please come here.
I will swallow you whole if I can."

The Fish said, "Tuck in, but before you begin,
Say, have you tasted a man?"

"Are men scrummy to eat?" said the Whale. "Are they sweet?"
The Fish said, "They're simply the best!

They're nubbly to nibble, but still, you will dribble,
And there's one right now, in the west."

The Whale shouted, "Oi! This is only a boy!
Though I guess even small ones are yum.

But he's shrimpy to chew, so I'll eat that boat too!"
And he gulped every bit in his tum.

Then how that boy jumped!
How he thumped! How he bumped!
How he banged and he clanged with a kick!

How he leapt
and he prowled!

How he crept!
How he growled!

And he made that old Whale go, "Er . . .

. . . Hic!"

"Help!" he said. "Quick! All these hics make me sick!"
"Let him go," said the Fish. "Or you'll burst."
But that clever young man had a cunning new plan,
And he said, "You must take me home first."

So the Whale swam some more
  till he reached a far shore,
While the boy tore his
  boat into bits.

Then he rammed that small boat
  down the Whale's greedy throat,
And he shouted, "Now see if that fits!"

"I can't eat!" said the Whale, and he turned deathly pale,
"As this boat in my throat is now stuck!"
But the boy, safely out, gave a chortle and shout,
And the Fish and the boy said, "Tough luck!"

"The skate and his mate," sang the Whale, "both taste great,
And the twirliest, swirliest eels.
But because of my greed, I will now have to feed
On the tiddliest bits for my meals."

So that is the tale of why whopping huge whales
Never gobble up people for dinner.
Their mouths are quite vast, but a child can't get past
As their throats are so very much thinner.

How the Camel got his Hump

Camels are grumpy and lumpy and bumpy,
They really do rather stand out.
Their backs were once straight,
and they thought that looked great!
But here's how their humps came about . . .

When the world was still new, there was plenty to do
For the creatures who lived in the sand.
But the Camel just sat, eating this, eating that,
Quite the laziest lump in the land!

"Humph, humph, humpety-humph!"
Was all that the Camel would say.
"Humph, humph, humpety-humph!"
And he simply sat snoozing all day.

Then one Monday morning a Horse came along,
And she said, "Will you come out and trot?
Don't laze in the sun – there is work to be done!"

But of course, that old Camel would not.

"Humph, humph, humpety-humph!"
The Camel said, shaking his head.
So the Horse pulled its load down the long desert road
While the Camel just went back to bed.

Then along came a Dog, who said, "Phew! What a slog!
There is so much to carry and fetch!
This work could be quick if you helped with these sticks,
And you're taller than me – you can stretch."

But "Humph, humph, humpety-humph!"
The Camel replied with a groan.
And he just lounged around, while down there on the ground
That poor Dog did the work on his own.

Then an Ox with a plough came along and said, "Now,
A big creature like you is so strong!
How light this will seem if we work as a team!
So please – help me pull it along."

Then the Horse, Dog and Ox said, "That Camel's a pest!"
"He's a grump!" "He's a lump!" "He's a pain!"
"This is all so unfair!" "Camel just doesn't care!"
So they went to their boss to complain.

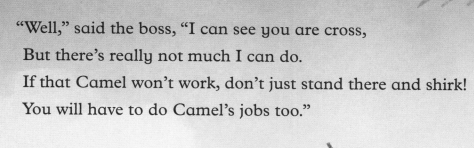

"Well," said the boss, "I can see you are cross,
But there's really not much I can do.
If that Camel won't work, don't just stand there and shirk!
You will have to do Camel's jobs too."

"Humph, humph, humpety-humph!"
The Camel replied with a grin.
But just as he spoke, in a PUFF
came some smoke . . .

35

And there stood a magical Djinn.

"Camel," he said, with a shake of his head,
"Now get off your lazy old rump!
 And if you do not, here's a spell that I've got:
 I will give you a humpety . . .

. . . hump!"

"My back!" Camel yelled. "Oh just look how it's swelled!"
But the Djinn said, "There's no time to laze!
It doesn't look dandy, but still, a hump's handy:
Your food can be stored there for days!"

37

So for days Camel huffed, and he panted and puffed,
Though he never once needed to eat.
And the Dog, Ox and Horse had a snooze, for of course
They were tired in that toe-roasting heat.

"I suppose," Camel thought, "that a hump of this sort
    Is quite useful for food on the go."
    But still Camel grumbled, and muttered and mumbled,
    And what was that word – do you know?

"Humph, humph, humpety-humph!"
That's all that a camel will say.
So camels are grumpy and lumpy and bumpy
And have a big hump to this day.

How the Rhinoceros got his Skin

The Rhino's grey skin was once smooth and quite thin,
And had buttons that fastened below.
But now it's all rumpled and thickish and crumpled,
And here's how that came to be so . . .

A wise man once sat in the shade of his hat
On the shores of the rippling Red Sea,
And he said, "I will bake a splendiferous cake
For my breakfast, my lunch and my tea."

"My cake," the man cried,
    "will be two whole feet wide,
And have sugar and currants inside it.
So plumptious! So sweet!
    And so scrumptious to eat!"

But then, whoops . . .

. . . someone else came and spied it.

That Rhino came charging and bashing and barging,
And chuckling and chortling with glee.
"That cake looks divine – oh, and now it's all mine!
Oh yes, every last bite is for me!"

How he slobbered and slurped! How he gobbled and burped!
How he stomped with his tum full of cake!

But the man muttered, "*Taking* a piece of my *baking*
Is really a dreadful mistake."

"He's a bad-mannered bandit! I really can't stand it!
I'll teach a few things to that Rhino!"
So he plotted and planned as he sat in the sand . . .
Then he suddenly shouted, "I know!"

And he waited for days in the warm desert haze
Till the sun came up tum-toasting hot.
Then he did a small dance, saying, "This is my chance
For my cunning and cleverest plot!"

The sun was so sizzling the creatures were frizzling,
And everyone tried to keep cool.
But the man simply sat in the shade of his hat
Till that Rhino stomped down to the pool.

The Rhino came charging and bashing and barging,
And stripped off his lovely smooth skin.
Then splishing and splashing and slamming and crashing
He went to the sea and dived in.

Then the man, with a smile that was long as a mile,
Gave that skin a good jostle and shake.
And he stuffed it and crammed it and filled it and rammed it
With currants and crumbs from his cake!

The Rhino got dressed. Then his back and his chest
And his tum and his legs started twitching.
He scratched and he rubbed and he scritched and he scrubbed,
Then he shouted out loudly, "I'm ITCHING!"

"I'm tickling!" he shouted. "I'm prickling!" he shouted,
And scratched himself quicker and quicker.

Then he wallowed and rolled till his skin hung in folds
And it soon became thicker and thicker.

"Too bad!" the man said with a shake of his head
As he watched that beast bellow and bawl.
"You were ever so rude when you took all my food –
No, you don't have good manners AT ALL."

So that's why a rhino looks chunky and clunky:
It's all on account of that cake.
As stealing and taking a piece of nice baking
Is really a dreadful mistake.

The Elephant's Child

Elephant trunks are such curious things:
Strongish and longish and grey.
But do you suppose that an elephant's nose
Was always exactly this way?

The Elephant's Child was a sweet-looking thing
With a nose like a squashed little boot.
But despite all of that, this young beast was a brat,
And nobody thought he was cute.

This Elephant had lots of questions, you see.
He'd prod and he'd pester and pry.

He chattered a lot and asked, "How, when and what?"
And he always whined, "Why, why, why, WHY?"

"Aunty Giraffe," the Elephant said.
"Why is your skin strangely spotty?"
   But Giraffe simply said,
      as she tossed her tall head,
"Go away! You are driving me dotty!"

"Uncle Baboon," the Elephant said.
"Why is your bottom so rosy?"
 But Baboon said, "Clear out! I don't want you about!
 Now buzz off, and stop being nosy!"

Then the Elephant thought of a new thing to ask:
"What does a Crocodile eat?"
 But no one replied, though he questioned and tried,
 "Do crocs crunch on veggies or meat?"

"Then I'll find out myself," said the Elephant's Child,
And he stomped through the trees – thump, thump, THUD.
Then he came to a lake, where he found a small Snake
Lying coiled in the boggish brown mud.

"Wakey-wake, Snakey," the Elephant cried.
"Listen, have you seen a croc?"
The Snake said "Oh yessssss, he's around here, I guesssssss.
He tends to hang out by that rock."

The Elephant searched all around for the Croc
In the slush and the mush of the bog.
Then he said, "Nothing here," and he plonked his large rear
By the side of a wrinkled old log.

"Nobody answers my questions," he sighed.
"So what do crocs eat? Let me think."
Then a voice said, "Ask *me* what a croc scoffs for tea."

And the log gave a sinister wink.

"You're not a log!" the Elephant cried
As the Crocodile said, "Do step near.
Oh my precious young sweet, you will know what I eat
When I whisper some words in your ear."

Closer and closer the Elephant came,
While the Crocodile stretched out his toes . . .
Then the Croc said, "Now YOU would be lovely to chew!"
And he bit on the Elephant's nose.

"Oh, you'll taste so divine," said the Croc with a crunch,
"I will gobble you up till I'm full."
Then the Elephant wailed as he floundered and flailed,
But the Snake yelled, "Stop howling, and PULL!"

So the Elephant pulled, and the Crocodile pulled,
And they heaved and they tugged to and fro.
Then the Crocodile yanked, and the Elephant yanked,
Till the Snake said, "Let ME have a go."

The Snake coiled tight round the Elephant's legs,
And she helped him with all of her strength.

The Crocodile stopped. The Elephant flopped.
Then he cried, "My poor nose! What a length!"

"I'll bathe it in water," the Elephant sniffed.
"And I'll stay sitting here till it's shrunk."
So he waited for days in the hot jungle haze,
But it seemed that he STILL had a trunk.

"Never mind," said the Snake, as the Elephant sobbed.
"A trunk is quite useful, you see.
You can whisk off that fly – just give it a try –
And reach down that fruit from the tree."

The Elephant found that the Snake was quite right:
His nose could go *swish* and go *swing*.
It could dangle and stretch, it could grab, it could fetch –
Yes, a trunk was a wonderful thing!

So that is why elephants' trunks are so strange,
So strongish and longish and grey.
But I tend to suppose that each elephant knows
That its nose is much better that way.

The Cat that Walked by Himself

Cats can be cuddly and friendly,
And purr as they sit on your chair.
So why do they sometimes ignore you,
And act like you're simply not there?

When the world was a far-reaching forest,
Where trees grew terrifically tall,
The animals played in the sun-speckled shade
And they didn't like humans at all.

The Dog was wild, and the Horse was wild,
And also the little brown Bat.
The Cow was wild, and the Sheep was wild,
But wildest of all was the Cat.

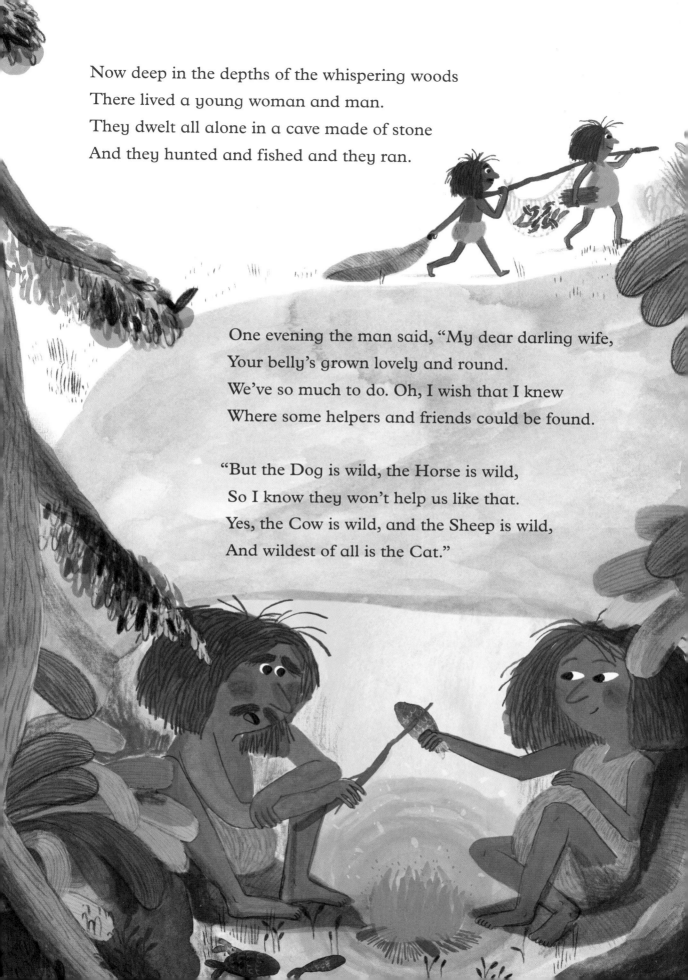

Now deep in the depths of the whispering woods
There lived a young woman and man.
They dwelt all alone in a cave made of stone
And they hunted and fished and they ran.

One evening the man said, "My dear darling wife,
Your belly's grown lovely and round.
We've so much to do. Oh, I wish that I knew
Where some helpers and friends could be found.

"But the Dog is wild, the Horse is wild,
So I know they won't help us like that.
Yes, the Cow is wild, and the Sheep is wild,
And wildest of all is the Cat."

Later that night in the shivery shade,
The woman put sticks on the fire.
She sang in the dark, and her song made a spark
Till the flames rose up higher and higher.

Then the Horse drew near, and the Dog drew near,
And they said, "What strange magic is that?"
The Cow drew near, and the Sheep drew near,
"But I'm far too wild," said the Cat.

"Please," said the Dog, "may I chew these nice bones?"
The woman said, "Yes, if you want.
But here is the deal: you will each get a meal
If you'll help us to fetch and to hunt."

The Horse said, "Oh" and the Cow said "Oh!"
As the Dog sat and ate on the mat.
The Sheep said, "Oh!" but the Cat said, "So?
I will always be wild, and that's that."

"I'll go and get Dog,"
    said the Horse the next day,
"For she seems to be under a spell.
    Our friend has been tamed,
    and she should be ashamed.
    But wait – what's that glorious smell?"

"It's lovely fresh grass," the woman called out.
"So do come inside for a snack.
  Now here is the deal: you will each get a meal
  If you let us have rides on your back."

The Cow said, "Oh!" and the Sheep said, "Oh!"
As the Horse stood and ate on the mat.
But the Cat said, "So?" and the Cat said, "I know
I will always be wild, and that's that."

Then the Cow and the Sheep both went to the cave,
And the woman said, "Eat till you're full.
But here is the deal: you will each get a meal
If you promise your milk and your wool."

So the Dog was tamed, and the Horse was tamed,
And they lived in the cave, just like that.
The Cow was tamed, and the Sheep was tamed.
"But I'll always be wild," said the Cat.

Now one winter morning the Cat sniffed the breeze,
Saying, "Mmm, I smell milk from the cow!
It's warm and it's white, it's a creamy delight!
I would so love to drink some – but how?"

So he went to the woman and purred, "Why, hello!
You are ever so wise and so pretty.
Do let me come in, to warm my cold skin,
And give me some milk. Have some pity!"

The Dog said, "Eh?" and the Horse said, "Neigh?"
But the woman just said as she sat:
"The Cow's been tamed, and the Sheep's been tamed,
But you are too wild, and that's that."

Then just as the Cat was turning to leave,
The woman said, "Learn to behave.
Mend your wild ways, and earn my good praise,
Then I'll let you come into the cave."

"If you praise me again, can I sit by the fire?
Will you give me some milk?" the Cat mewed.
But the woman just laughed. "Oh Cat, don't be daft!
Now shoo! You're too wild and too rude."

So away he crept, and away he leapt,
That wild and contemptuous Cat.
Away he prowled, and away he growled:
"I'll always be wild, and that's that."

Then one sunny morning, when spring filled the air,
The Bat came and called, "Cat, so wild!
Listen up well, I've got news I can tell:
The woman and man have a child!"

"Oh!" cried the Cat. "I must see them at once!"
And he leapt with a proud little prance.
"Babies like fur, and soft things that purr.
I will hurry, as this is my chance!"

"They'll be pleased and surprised,
   I'll be praised, I'll be prized,
   Then I'll sit by the fire," said the Cat.
"I'll drink, and I'll eat the most succulent meat,
   But I'll still be quite wild, and that's that."

The baby was bawling with all of her might.
How she screamed! How she screeched! How she wriggled!
But she saw the soft Cat, and she gave him a pat,
Then she stroked him, and poked him, and giggled.

"Oh!" said the woman. "Thank goodness for that!
What creature has cheered up my child?
I'm pleased and amazed, let that creature be praised!"
And she glanced at her baby and smiled.

The baby said, "Coo!" The woman said "Who?"
Then she looked, and she said, "Oh, it's Cat.
Well, come in the cave, and make sure you behave.
But I won't let you sit, and that's that."

The next day the baby was crying again
As the woman sat spinning Sheep's wool.
But the Cat tossed his head, then he bit at the thread,
And he gave it a tug and a pull.

Then he patted it, batted it, tore it and tattered it,
Chasing the wool round the flowers.
He crawled and he crept and he sprang and he leapt,
And the baby sat clapping for hours.

The baby said, "Coo!" The woman said, "Who?"
Then she looked and she said, "Thank you, Cat.
I suppose you may sit by the fire for a bit,
But you won't drink the milk, and that's that."

"Cat," said the woman, "you're useful, I know,
  But you're still far too wild for this place."
"Really?" said Cat, as he caught a brown rat.
"Just think of the things that I chase!"

"Ha!" said the woman. "I see you are wise,
  So come to the fireside and drink.
  We both made a deal, so here is your meal."
  But she noticed the Dog give a wink.

The Cat went *lick*, his tail went *flick*,
  And it finished the milk, just like that.
"What do I care about Dog over there?
  I'm the wisest of all," said the Cat.

But at this the Dog leapt, and she snarled at the Cat:
"You have not made a bargain with ME.
Remember, I fight, and I bark and I bite!"
And she chased the Cat straight up a tree.

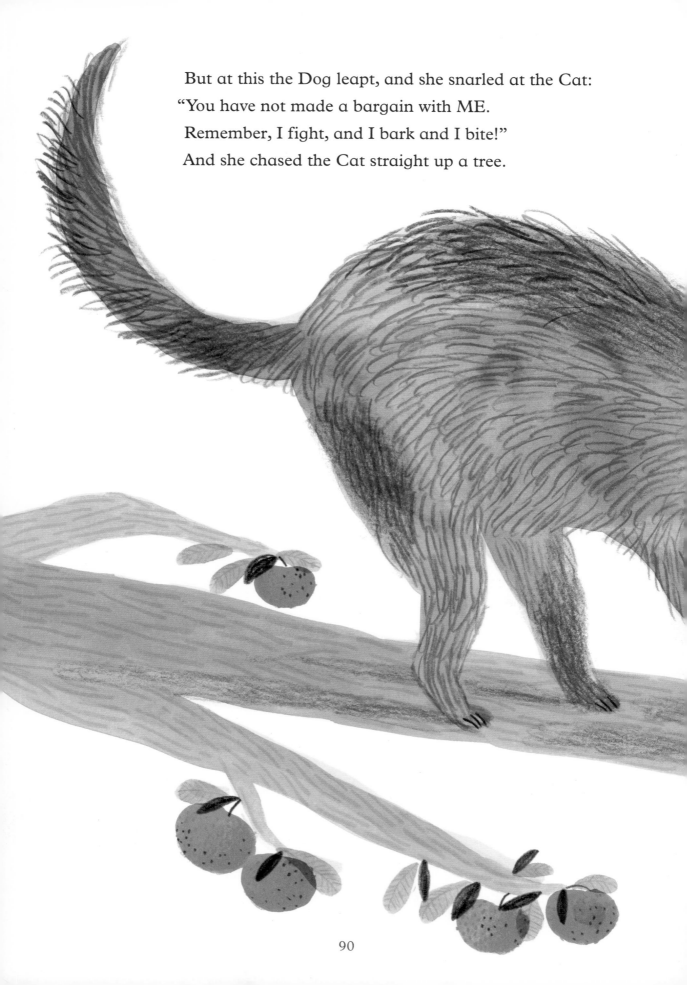

"So you think you walk where you like?" said the Dog.
"You think you can choose what to do?

Yes, you're ever so wild," said Dog as she smiled.
"However, I'm bigger than YOU."

But the Cat shut his eyes, looking scornful and wise,

And he said not a word in reply.

He stretched out the claws on his little soft paws,

And disdainfully swatted a fly.

For the Dog was wild, the Horse was wild,

And so was the little brown Bat.

The Cow was wild, and the Sheep was wild,

But who is *still* wild? Yes, the Cat.